THIS CANDLEWICK BOOK BELONGS TO:

_____

_____

_____

For Will, who asked us this question when he was two
and has not stopped asking intriguing questions since.
With love and wokkas from Auntie Boo.
E. B.

For Luke
R. C.

Text copyright © 2009 by Elizabeth Bluemle
Illustrations copyright © 2009 by Randy Cecil

First paperback edition 2012

The Library of Congress has cataloged the hardcover edition as follows:

Bluemle, Elizabeth.
How do you wokka-wokka? / Elizabeth Bluemle ;
illustrated by Randy Cecil. —1st ed.
p.   cm.
Summary: A young boy who likes to "wokka-wokka, shimmy-shake, and shocka-shocka"
gathers his neighbors together for a surprise celebration.
ISBN 978-0-7636-3228-1 (hardcover)
[1. Stories in rhyme. 2. Dance—Fiction. 3. Neighbors—Fiction. 4. Parties—Fiction.]   I. Cecil, Randy, ill. II. Title.
PZ8.3.B59854Ho 2009
[E]—dc22   20080277152

ISBN 978-0-7636-6085-7 (paperback)

18 19 CCP 10 9 8 7 6

Printed in Shenzhen, Guangdong, China

This book was typeset in Aunt Mildred.
The illustrations were done in oil.

Candlewick Press
99 Dover Street
Somerville, Massachusetts 02144

visit us at www.candlewick.com

How Do You Wokka-Wokka?

Elizabeth Bluemle

illustrated by Randy Cecil

CANDLEWICK PRESS

Some days you wake up
and you just gotta wokka—

Say "HEY!" to your neighbors
up and down the blocka

wammy-lammy-wotcha-hoo.
Do your funky wokka,
get your dance on.

How do you wokka-wokka?

I wokka-wokka
like flamingos
in a flocka–

croakie-yocka

leggy-longy

pinky-hoppa-hoppa

How do you wokka-wokka?

I wokka like a
mariachi with
maracas—

chipi-chipi

chaba-cha-cha

shake-a-the-maracas

Hey, let's wokka-wokka,
shimmy-shake, and shocka-shocka!

Everybody dance now in your
shiny shoes and socka-socka.

You can always wokka
in your own wokka way.

Won't you come out with me
on this fine old wokka day?

How do you wokka-wokka?

I wokka-wokka
like a clock
go ticka-tocka–

pitta-patta

time-no-matta

pick-pock-ticka-tocka

flip-a-floppa

off-the-docka

put-me-back-in-wata-wata

Hey, let's wokka-wokka,
shimmy-shake, and shocka-shocka!

Time to get a move-on in your
shiny shoes and socka-socka.

Everybody wokka in their own crazy way.

Won't you wokka with me on this fine old sunny day?

How do YOU wokka-wokka?

I wokka-wokka
at your door go
knocka-knocka–

rap-bap

biddly-ap

open-up-and-boppa

WE wokka-wokka like
a party on the blocka!

Shacka-racka
daddly-acka

cotton-candy

snacka-snacka.

Nobody wokkas
in the same wokka way.

It's a wokka-wokka party
each and every wokka day!

We all gonna rocka

Elizabeth Bluemle is the author of *Dogs on the Bed*, illustrated by Anne Wilsdorf, and *My Father the Dog*, illustrated by Randy Cecil. About this book, she says, "When my nephew, Will, was two, he started asking us, 'How do you wokka-wokka?' He knew what he meant, but we didn't, so we answered him with funny dance moves. The way he brought people of every generation joyfully together with one simple, silly question grew into this book." Elizabeth Bluemle lives in Vermont, where she co-owns the Flying Pig Bookstore in Shelburne.

Randy Cecil is the author-illustrator of *Gator* and *Duck*, which *School Library Journal* called "a beautifully realized friendship story." In addition to *My Father the Dog* by Elizabeth Bluemle, he has illustrated several other books, including *Brontorina* by James Howe, *We've All Got Bellybuttons!* by David Martin, and *Looking for a Moose* by Phyllis Root. He lives in Houston, Texas.